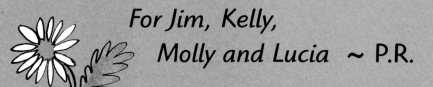

For Jim, Kelly,
Molly and Lucia ~ P.R.

For Nick ~ S.H.

First published 1996 by Walker Books Ltd
87 Vauxhall Walk, London SE11 5HJ

10 9 8 7 6 5 4 3 2 1

Text © 1996 Phyllis Root
Illustrations © 1996 Sue Heap

Printed in Hong Kong

This book has been typeset in Highlander Book.

British Library Cataloguing in Publication Data
A catalogue record for this book
is available from the British Library.

ISBN 0-7445-4072-0

THE HUNGRY MONSTER

Written by
Phyllis Root

Illustrated by
Sue Heap

Earth MAP

WALKER BOOKS
AND SUBSIDIARIES
LONDON • BOSTON • SYDNEY

A rocket came to Planet Earth.
Out stepped a monster.

"HUNGRY!" roared the monster.

The monster
saw a daisy.
"YUM!" said the monster.

The monster tasted
the daisy.

"REALLY HUNGRY!"
roared the monster.
The monster saw a rock.
"YUM!" said the monster.

The monster tasted
the rock.

"YUCK!"
said the
monster.

"REALLY, REALLY HUNGRY!"
roared the monster.
The monster saw a tree.
"YUM!" said the monster.

The monster tasted the tree.

"YUCK!" said the monster.

"REALLY, REALLY, REALLY HUNGRY!" roared the monster.

The monster
saw a girl...

"YUM!" said the monster.

"**YIKES!**" said the girl.
"**Have a banana.**"

The monster ate the banana,
skin and all.

"**YUCK!**" said the girl.